A Mouse in My House

A Mouse in My House

by
Nancy Van Laan

pictures by
Marjorie Priceman

A TRUMPET CLUB SPECIAL EDITION

A mouse is in my house,
and it's small, gray, and furry.
There's a mouse in my house,
and it acts like me.

It climbs and it wriggles
as it nibbles and it giggles.
There's a mouse in my house,
only I can see.

A cat is in my house,
and it's black like a shadow.
There's a cat in my house,
and it acts like me.

It yowls and it hisses
as it pounces and it misses.
There's a cat in my house,
only I can see.

A dog is in my house,
and it's brown like a puddle.
There's a dog in my house,
and it acts like me.

It scatters all my toys,
and it makes a lot of noise.
There's a dog in my house,
only I can see.

A snake is in my house,
and it's green like a bean.
There's a snake in my house,
and it acts like me.

Silently it hides
as it slithers and it slides.
There's a snake in my house,
only I can see.

A bug is in my house,
and it's red and it's angry.
There's a bug in my house,
and it acts like me.

It itches and it scratches
when it has to wear what matches.
There's a bug in my house,
only I can see.

A fish is in my house,
and it's blue and it's slippery.
There's a fish in my house,
and it acts like me.

It dives and it crashes
as it bubbles and it splashes.
There's a fish in my house,
only I can see.

An ape is in my house,
and it's tan and it's scraggly.
There's an ape in my house,
and it acts like me.

It laughs when it pleases
as it clowns and it teases.
There's an ape in my house,
only I can see.

A bear is in my house,
and it's white and it's shaggy.
There's a bear in my house,
and it acts like me.

It grumbles and it thumps
as it bumbles and it bumps.
There's a bear in my house,
only I can see.

A pig is in my house,
and it's pink like a posy.
There's a pig in my house,
and it acts like me.

It chomps and it burps
as it begs for two desserts.
There's a pig in my house,
only I can see.

A lion is in my house,
and it's yellow and it's clumsy.
There's a lion in my house,
and it acts like me.

It scribbles with its claws,
spills the paint, and glues its paws.
There's a lion in my house,
only I can see.

A zoo is in my house,
and it's loud and it's noisy.

There's a zoo in my house,

and the zoo is ME!

For my sister, Julie,
and Frank, Michelle, Mike, and Chris
—N.V.L.

For Bill
—M.P.

Published by The Trumpet Club
666 Fifth Avenue, New York, New York 10103

Text copyright © 1990 by Nancy Van Laan
Illustrations copyright © 1990 by Marjorie Priceman

ISBN: 0-440-84617-X

This edition published by arrangement
with Alfred A. Knopf, Inc., a division
of Random House, Inc.
Book design by Elizabeth Hardie
Printed in the United States of America
October 1991

10 9 8 7 6 5 4 3 2 1
UPC